Holt, Rinehart and Winston, Inc. New York, Toronto, London, Sydney

Copyright © 1970 by Holt, Rinehart and Winston, Inc. Library of Congress Catalog Number: 77-109208   SBN: 03-084599-8. Printed in the United States of America   Published simultaneously in Canada.

MY DAYS ARE MADE OF BUTTERFLIES

by Sano M. Galea'i Fa'apouli
adapted by Bill Martin, Jr.
with pictures by Vic Herman

*My days are made of butterflies
that gather on the melon vine,*

My days are made of oranges
that ripen in the warm sunshine,

*My days are made of sudden rains
that drench the yard with happiness,*

My days are made of hungry hawks
that stalk the desert wilderness,

My days are made of working

with my father planting sugar beets,

My days are made of herding lambs

that wander from our flock of sheep,

My days are made of singing
in the village at fiesta time,

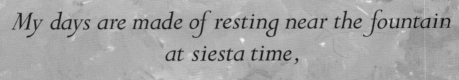

*My days are made of resting near the fountain
at siesta time,*

My days are made of ling'ring in the kitchen
while my mother cooks,

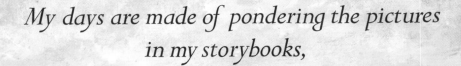

My days are made of pondering the pictures in my storybooks,

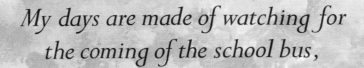

My days are made of watching for
the coming of the school bus,

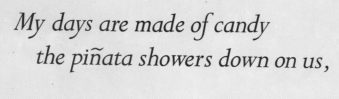

My days are made of candy
the piñata showers down on us,

Then, when the sun slips down behind the mountains
and the silent owl on the nightwind wings,

I lie looking at the quiet stars

and wonder what tomorrow brings.

VIC HERMAN